Evie's Magic Bracelet

Read more in the Evie's Magic Bracelet series!

Evie's Magic Bracelet

The Enchanted Puppy

JESSICA ENNIS-HILL
and Elen Caldecott

Illustrated by
Erica-Jane Waters

Hodder
Children's
Books

HODDER CHILDREN'S BOOKS

First published in Great Britain in 2017 by Hodder and Stoughton

1 3 5 7 9 10 8 6 4 2

A CIP catalogue record for this book
is available from the British Library.

ISBN 978 1 444 93440 3

Printed and bound in Great Britain by Clays Ltd, St Ives plc

The paper and board used in this book
are made from wood from responsible sources

Hodder Children's Books
An imprint of
Hachette Children's Group
Part of Hodder and Stoughton
Carmelite House
50 Victoria Embankment
London EC4Y 0DZ

An Hachette UK Company
www.hachette.co.uk

www.hachettechildrens.co.uk

Chapter 1

Evie Hall squinted at the glittery dust motes that danced beneath her skylight. Was it sunshine, or magic? Sunshine or magic? It was hard to tell. Grandma Iris would know. But Grandma Iris was thousands of miles away in Jamaica. She had sent Evie an amazing, fantabulous bracelet that helped her see magic and talk to animals. But the charm had worn off and now the bracelet was just a pretty trinket on Evie's wrist. Actually, a pretty grimy trinket by now – she hadn't taken it off, not even when she slept. Evie sighed. Well, the magic had been fun while it lasted.

'Evie!' Dad's voice boomed up the stairs. 'Get a wriggle on!'

Oh! School! Rats. She'd been so busy staring at maybe-magic that she'd forgotten all about getting ready. Luckily, her book bag and shoes were right where she'd left them, neatly arranged beside her chair. She pulled on her shoes quickly and clattered out of her attic bedroom down to the hall.

Dad stood at the bottom of the stairs. He held something small, cradled in his huge hands. 'The post came while you were daydreaming,' Dad said with a grin. 'There's something here for you.'

For her? She did a little dance of joy. Could it be from Grandma Iris?

Dad held out the beautifully wrapped package. Evie saw the handwriting. It was! It was from Grandma Iris. 'Thank you,' she grinned at Dad.

'Be quick,' he said, 'we leave in two minutes.'

She sat on the bottom step while Dad went to see what was keeping her little sister, Lily. Myla the dog thumped her tail hopefully, in case the pretty box was full of dog treats.

'Sorry, Myla, but Grandma Iris only sends pooch chocs at Christmas. This one's for me.'

Myla's ears drooped miserably.

Evie untied the ribbon and let the tissue paper fall open.

'Oh!' she gasped. It was another bracelet. This time silk threads wove around tiny shells that glimmered and glistened as she lifted it free. Was Dad watching? She peered around the banister. No. He was trying to get Lily to put her shoes on, but she could only find one of them. Evie swapped her old bracelet for the new one quickly, before the mystery of the lost shoe was solved.

Was the magic back? She put her face right up to Myla's. 'How are you doing today?' she asked.

Myla licked her, right on the chops.

'Eww! Gross!' Evie said, wiping her face on the back of her sleeve. Well, Myla wasn't talking. Maybe this bracelet was just a bracelet after all. Wait. Grandma Iris had sent a note last time, was there one this time? She pushed aside the tissue paper, and then she saw it.

'With this gift there will unfold
Three days of joy and magic's gold.
The sparkle won't be just for you,
We're on the move, we'll feel brand new!'

Great, more riddles. Grandma Iris liked to be tricksy. But Evie would work it out. She would be tricksy too. She pulled down the sleeve of her jumper, just as Lily

barrelled down the hallway.

'School time!' Lily shouted. 'Last one there's a stink-head.'

Evie left the house, wondering about Grandma Iris' words. What could she mean?

Starrow Junior School was always busy as a beehive first thing in the morning. Parents with prams, kids on scooters and bikes, teachers carrying bags-for-life stuffed full of books, all headed through the gates. Evie kept a careful lookout for any signs of magic. Last time seagulls had talked and a unicorn had appeared during a paper chase. Was there any sign of it with this bracelet?

There!

She saw a bright streak of gold shooting like a rainbow as a toddler swung between his parents – 'Whee!' And another arc, as a boy threw his arms around his mum. The bracelet was working! Magic was definitely back! She couldn't wait to tell her two friends, Isabelle and Ryan.

She said goodbye to Dad, a little distractedly, then made her way to the Year 6 classroom. Miss Williams was setting up the whiteboard and the class chattered like a beck in full flood.

Evie skipped towards Isabelle and Ryan. When she was close, she pulled up the edge of her sleeve, without saying a word.

They both knew exactly what she was

9

showing them – they had joined in her previous adventure.

'Good old Grandma Iris!' Isabelle whispered.

'What does it do?' Ryan asked.

'I don't know yet. The note said we were "on the move", so maybe it will transport us somewhere fun,' Evie suggested.

Isabelle thumped her desk excitedly. 'Florida! Can it take us to Disney World? Or Arizona? I've always wanted to see the desert. No, wait, New York!' She finished with a dramatic drumroll.

'Isabelle Carter!' Miss Williams snapped. 'This is not band practice. Less of that noise, please.'

'Sorry, Miss,' Isabelle grinned.

Evie settled into her seat, near the window, as lessons began. She took out her pencil case and turned to a new page in her exercise book. But she wasn't really listening to Miss Williams.

What did her new bracelet do? Something to do with moving, that's what Grandma Iris' note had said.

She tapped the tip of her pencil gently against her book as she thought.

Miss Williams was saying something about running in the corridors.

Evie's left hand wandered, almost of its own accord, to her right wrist, where the bracelet was hidden away. She felt the tiny shells under her sleeve. Without thinking, she twisted the band around her wrist. A second time. A third.

Suddenly a sinuous snake of gold light shone along her arm.

Magic!

She tried to cover it with her left hand, but the light seeped between her fingers. Her eyes shot to Miss Williams – had she noticed? No. She was still speaking. And it was nearly impossible for grown-ups to see magic, anyway. It was easier for children. Evie's glance darted around the room. Was anyone watching? Yes. Isabelle and Ryan had both noticed the light – they were able to see magic too. Isabelle was grinning in delight. Ryan looked more frightened.

Her heart pounded as the magic flowed around and around her arm. It slipped down her wrist and along her fingers. It flowed into her pencil.

Her pencil jerked out of her hand.

It stood, upright, on her desk.

The magic light faded. But the pencil was

carefully balanced, all by itself, on its point, like a ballerina on tiptoes.

Evie stayed very, very still.

But the pencil didn't.

In what looked a lot like delight at suddenly being able to do its own thing, the pencil dashed, spun, waltzed and sailed across the open page. It left swoops and dashes, like skates marking an ice rink.

Then, as if happy with the dark marks it had made on the paper, it leapt off the page and began to dance across her desk! It left thick black marks behind it on the wood.

Evie finally found she could move.

She grabbed for the pencil, but it jumped away, bouncing on to the floor and rolling away, under a bookcase.

Miss Williams felt silent at the sudden noise. Then, she noticed the total mess that the pencil had left behind.

'Evie Hall,' Miss Williams said in horror. 'What on earth have you done to your desk?'

Chapter 2

Evie raised her head slowly to see Miss Williams looming above her. Miss Williams' eyes were firmly fixed on the black marks that streaked across her exercise book and then across the desk.

'I'm sorry,' Evie said. She could feel her cheeks burn as she realised what Miss

Williams must be thinking – that she had deliberately scribbled all over her own desk. She'd never do such a thing! But she couldn't say that the pencil did it – who would believe her? Only Ryan and Isabelle. Miss Williams? Never.

'I'd not have thought it of you,' Miss Williams said. 'You're normally such a sensible girl. What's gotten into you?'

What could she say?

Nothing.

Evie bit her lip.

'It was me, Miss!' Isabelle called. She held her arm poker straight in the air and looked fearless.

'What?' Miss Williams sounded confused.

'I did it,' Isabelle insisted. 'For a joke.
When you were setting up the whiteboard.
I got up and scribbled all over Evie's things.
I was being silly.'

'You were being very silly,' Miss Williams
agreed coldly.

19

Why was Isabelle taking the blame? It didn't make sense, she'd get into trouble and it would be Evie's fault. Well, it would be the magical pencil's fault, but that was sort of the same thing. She couldn't let that happen. She had to be brave.

Evie's heart was thumping hard, but she had to speak up. 'It wasn't Isabelle, Miss. It was me.'

Miss Williams tutted. 'Well, whoever it was, you're both being silly now. Which means you'll both have break time detention. No playing outside today. You can stay in the classroom and think about what you've done. And you can clean up that desk while you're at it.'

Evie felt her blush get even deeper – she hated getting into trouble.

But Isabelle caught her eye and gave her the cheekiest ghost of a wink.

'It was magic, wasn't it?' Isabelle demanded the moment that everyone went out at break time, leaving them alone in the classroom. She stood with her hands on her hips, her feet set apart, daring Evie to deny it.

Evie gave a tiny nod.

'Yesss! I *knew* it!' Isabelle clapped loudly.

'Hush! Miss Williams will hear and come and tell us off all over again.' Evie stood and walked over to the bookcase. She crouched on all fours and tried to squeeze her hand underneath. Where had that pencil got to? Was it still moving all by itself?

Isabelle sat on the edge of Evie's desk. 'So, the pencil came alive and did its own sketches?'

'If you can call them that,' Evie mumbled. The underneath of the bookshelf needed a sweep and her hand grabbed several disgusting dust bunnies.

'Yeah,' Isabelle said thoughtfully, 'that pencil's not going to win the school art competition, is it? You can't even tell what the sketch is meant to be. Still. This is fantastic news. Magic's back! And this time you can make things come to life. You can make vacuum cleaners do the cleaning by themselves! We'd make a fortune. Or, better still, you can make all of my big sister's clothes come alive and walk out of her wardrobe and into mine!'

Evie gave up on the pencil. Wherever it had gone to, she hoped it would be happy, because it had definitely run off. 'Isabelle,' Evie said. 'I have no idea why you are so excited. If you haven't noticed, we're in trouble. In detention.'

The sounds of everyone else screaming and laughing and tumbling around the playground floated up to them from below.

'We just have to make the best of it,' Isabelle replied. 'We'll get through today, then you can come back to my house and

23

see if we can turn Lizzie's skinny jeans into jumping beans that somehow, mysteriously jump their way into my room. Please? Please can we?' Isabelle batted her eyelashes in the way that worked so well with her parents.

Evie sighed. 'We can try out the magic. But not on Lizzie's things. And well away from other people watching. This has to stay secret.'

Isabelle leapt up and hugged Evie tightly. 'You're the best!' she said. 'We'll just get our letters signed then we can go out to the park, maybe. Try the magic on some dry old sticks, if that's what you want.'

'Letters?' Evie asked.

'Yeah, you know, the letters that Miss Williams will give us to take home to explain that we had a detention?'

'What?' Evie felt a knot form in the pit of her tummy.

'It's no big deal. Your mum or dad just has to sign it to say you told them what happened.'

The knot in her tummy twisted tight as Lizzie's skinny jeans. There was no way she could tell Mum and Dad that she'd got into trouble at school! They'd be so disappointed. They always wanted her to try her best and there was no way that they would think scribbling on her desk was in any way 'trying her best'. In fact, she was sure it was the exact opposite of trying her best.

'What's the matter?' Isabelle asked.

'I can't tell them,' Evie said. But she was going to have to. Keeping it a secret would just make it worse – they were bound to find out somehow. What was she going to do?

A huge grin spread over Isabelle's face. 'I know what you're going to do,' she said. 'This is a problem that you can solve with magic.'

'Is it?'

'Yes. Trust me, it's all going to be absolutely, totally and completely fine.'

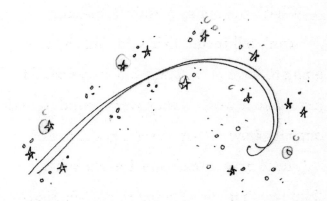

Chapter 3

'Do you want to hear my plan?' Isabelle
asked. She hopped up on to her desk and
swung her trainers back and forth.

Evie nodded. She was not at all sure
that Isabelle's plans were always the best.
Somehow, they always seemed to end up in
trouble, with Miss Williams telling them off,

or sprites chasing them, or *something*. But Isabelle was her friend, so she had to listen.

'You are supposed to give the letter to your parents. Which means you can't just put it in the bin, or "forget" to pass it on.' Isabelle made swift air-quotes. 'And anyway, you wouldn't do something like that.'

Isabelle was right. Evie would never deliberately lie to Mum or Dad. The idea was horrible. She fished around in her pencil case until she found a rubber and started scrubbing out the pencil's pesky prints.

'But!' Isabelle raised her finger like a judge giving a verdict. 'But, if the letter wandered off, all by itself, then you can hardly be blamed for that, can you?'

'Wandered off? What do you mean? Oh. You mean make it come alive, like the pencil?'

'Exactly. If it came alive, then it would take itself off to wherever bits of paper want to be. The library, I suppose. And it's gone for good out of your life. No more letter.'

Evie brushed away the tiny sausages of old rubber. 'But don't I have to give the letter back to Miss Williams? With Mum and Dad's signature on it?'

Isabelle made a spluttery-huffy noise. 'That's all right. She might nag once or twice, but that's all. Trust me. I've had loads of these letters.'

Trust Isabelle? She did, of course, but maybe not quite on absolutely everything.

'*And* you need to practise the magic before the bracelet runs out,' Isabelle added. 'I mean, one tiny slip of paper is probably a better thing to practise on than sticks in the park. Live sticks might hit people and you don't want that.'

Well, that was true. Making a piece of paper move was a nice, simple bit of magic. It wouldn't hurt anyone.

Isabelle leapt down off her desk and leaned so close that her hair tickled Evie's nose. 'Your mum and dad will never know a thing, and you won't even be telling them a little white lie. The paper will lose itself and you won't have broken any rules!'

Evie felt a tiny little tingle of excitement. Was Isabelle right? Could she really use magic to fix the problem and make sure Mum and Dad never found out?

The bell rang right at that moment. Children clattered back into the classroom, sweaty but smiling from break. Evie slipped silently back into her seat.

Miss Williams stopped to peer at her now-clean desk. 'That's better,' she said. 'Here, take this.' She held out the letter. It was no bigger than an envelope, but Evie knew it would set off an explosion in her house. She took it, still not sure what she was going to do. She could feel the bracelet resting lightly on her wrist.

Isabelle coughed sharply. Evie caught her eye. *Go on*, Isabelle's eyes urged, *do it*.

Could she?

More importantly, *should* she?

It couldn't hurt anyone. And if the letter lost itself, then she wasn't really lying to Mum and Dad if she didn't pass it on to them. Not *really*, really.

Yes, Evie decided, she was going to do it.

Evie smoothed the letter flat on her desk.
This was the first time she had deliberately
tried to do magic. She wasn't even sure
whether she could just do it on command,
or whether the bracelet had to *want* to do
it. She had both hands flat on the letter. She
was ready.

Move, she thought, *move.*

Nothing happened.

Evie sighed and looked up. Miss Williams
was going over a maths problem. She
had her back to the class. Everyone was
watching the whiteboard. She was droning

on about fractions and decimals and how many slices of cake someone would have if they had 75% of the cake. Evie thought that whoever it was would probably have a very sore tummy if they ate 75% of a cake.

The letter was a bigger problem than working out cake fractions.

Move, please, pretty please, she thought at the letter.

Nothing, not so much as a flutter.

What was she doing wrong? Perhaps she had to do something with the bracelet? Then she remembered, when the pencil came to life, she'd been twisting the bracelet. Yes! That was it! Evie grabbed the letter with her right hand, and held her bracelet with the

left. She turned it, once, twice, thr—

'Evie!' Miss Williams called her name.

She dropped the letter.

But her left hand finished the third turn.

Gold light shot from her wrist in a sudden
beam. It headed straight towards the reading
corner. An arc of light corkscrewed around
a toy kitten, bounced off the head of a
rubber duck, and then rushed into a
plush dog.

Then the light was gone.

What had just happened?

Had Miss Williams seen it?

'Evie Hall!' Miss Williams said. 'This
is the third time I've asked you for your
thoughts on this problem. What do we get if

we multiply these fractions?'

'Sorry, Miss,' Evie said, 'I don't know.'

Miss Williams sighed. 'Evie, I'm very surprised by your behaviour today. And disappointed.'

Ryan, with a worried look at Evie, put his hand in the air. 'I know, Miss!'

'Ryan? Excellent.' Miss Williams sounded so delighted that Ryan was listening that she forgot all about Evie.

Phew. She'd got away with it.

Just.

That was the last time she'd listen to one of Isabelle's bright ideas. She'd nearly got herself a second detention! From now on she was going to listen and work hard, and only use magic at weekends. It was going to be her new rule.

'Woof!'

The bark was so soft, so gentle, that Evie wondered whether she had imagined it. Then she saw movement in the reading corner: a tiny tail wagged, little ears pricked up. And there was more movement there! Wings flapping. And there! Whiskers twitching.

Uh-oh. Evie's eyebrows shot right up. The magic had worked, but not on the letter! It had worked on the soft toys in the reading corner!

Now, Year 6 had a real puppy, a real kitten and a real, live, waddling, quacking,

pecking duck in the corner of the classroom,

clambering over the soft cushions and

tumbling down the other side, exploring

their new world.

The toys had come to life.

No one else had noticed yet. But, as the

kitten stretched and tested its claws on a

cloth-bound edition of *Alice in Wonderland*, and the puppy sniffed at a battered copy of *James and the Giant Peach*, before lifting its leg and widdling on the spine, Evie knew it was only a matter of time.

Chapter 4

There were three live animals in Year 6's classroom and it was Evie's fault. What on earth was she going to do about this new palaver? *James and the Giant Peach* was never going to be the same again.

How long would it be before anyone noticed the petting zoo where the reading

corner used to be? She *had* to fix this,
and quick.

'So,' Miss Williams said, 'I'd like you all
to move into groups to look at questions six
and seven on the worksheet. Amira, please
pass the sheets around.'

Evie made a desperate lunge for Isabelle
and Ryan. She needed them in her group.
'Bagsie the reading corner!' she said loudly.
Hooking one friend on each arm like human
armbands, she dived behind the bookcase.

'This is an emergency!' she hissed at them.

'Is this a maths emergency?' Ryan asked.
'Because I don't do those.'

'No. A magic emergency,' Evie said. 'Look!'
She pointed at the kitten and the puppy,

and the duck. Isabelle blinked. The animals blinked back. The duck gave a soft quack.

'Are they real?' Ryan whispered. 'Where did they come from?'

'They're real now,' Evie replied urgently. 'Remember the toy kitten and dog, and the rubber duck. Well ...' she spread her hands at the animals, 'they aren't toys any more.'

'Oh, they're so cute!' Isabelle tried to scoop the duck into her arms. The duck had no interest in being cuddled. It squawked in alarm and flapped its wings. It rose up in the air indignantly and wobbled its way to the top of the bookcase.

'Great,' Evie sighed, looking up at the ruffled-looking bird.

'What was that noise?' Miss Williams asked, turning a steely gaze towards the corner.

'I just read question six,' Ryan said quickly. 'It made me squawk.'

The duck quacked again.

'Qu-rikey! Question seven is hard as well,' Isabelle added.

Luckily, at that moment, someone on the other side of the classroom snatched someone else's workbook and Miss Williams had to hurry over.

'Get that duck down,' Evie told Ryan, who was tallest.

The top of the bookshelf was beyond his reach. He leapt up. He came nowhere

close. He tried again. He was miles off. He took a few steps back, then rocked gently on his back foot working out his stride. Then he ran at the shelf from the side before arching and leaping into the air, his hand outstretched.

And missed the duck completely.

'Try this,' Isabelle said, handing him a stool.

He climbed up and reached for the bird. The duck pecked at his fingers curiously, as though he might have crumbs of bread.

'Ow!' he moaned. The duck flapped its wings and fluttered down to land on Ryan's head. 'Hey!' he said.

'It's because your hair looks like a nest,' Isabelle said.

'It does not!'

Alarmed by their raised voices, the duck fluttered straight back up to its high perch.

Meanwhile the kitten had dug its claws into a woollen blanket and tugged and kneaded and yanked until the wool was pulled in every direction, pinging away from the blanket like colourful spaghetti.

'Oh, no,' Isabelle said. 'Miss Williams' mum crocheted that blanket. Come on, Kitty, come away.' She tried to coax the kitten clear with a felt fish snatched from the pile of soft toys. But the kitten was having too much fun tearing into the blanket. It rolled on to its back so that it could put all four claws to the job.

'Evie!' Ryan said. 'You have to do something! Make them turn back into toys.'

That was exactly what she had to do.

She'd never tried to reverse magic before, but then, it was a morning for firsts. First detention, first time doing magic deliberately and now, first time undoing magic.

She could do this.

She looked at the puppy. It was a messy mix of straggly fur, with huge dark eyes. It was sitting neatly, watching them all. Its little tail flicked back and forth.

'I don't want to turn you back into a toy,' Evie said, 'but I have to.'

'Incoming!' Ryan called.

The duck swooped down from the shelf,
its legs splayed for a heavy landing. It
barrelled into the kitten and the two of them
rolled. Threads of coloured wool whipped
round, wrapping the two animals in a
rainbow net. The kitten hissed in alarm.

51

The duck quacked angrily.

The puppy thumped its tail.

'What on earth is going on?' Miss Williams asked.

Evie dropped to the ground, shielding the Battle of the Blanket with her body. Ryan kicked his bag, so that the puppy was in its shadow.

Isabelle beamed at Miss Williams. 'We're having beastly trouble with question six,' she said. 'Is there any way you could go over it with me one more time? Just for luck?'

Miss Williams eyed the ceiling, but then nodded. 'Come here, Isabelle. Where I can keep an eye on you.'

Isabelle followed Miss Williams out of the reading corner.

With Miss Williams back at her desk, Evie lifted the blanket. The kitten and duck had stopped squabbling, mostly because they had gotten too tangled in the wool to move.

'Right,' Evie said. She reached out to stroke the kitten's paw. It purred softly. She tried to relax; Dad always said that no problem was ever fixed by worrying. With the kitten's paw between the pads of her fingers, she twisted the bracelet on her arm, once, twice, three times …

… gold light flowed gently down her wrist and twirled around the sleepy kitten, wrapping it in a soft, golden haze. The kitten yawned and Evie saw its tiny, pink tongue flick ... and then it was just a soft toy again, tangled in wool.

She'd done it. She'd worked magic.

A bubble of glee burst inside her, but she had to stay relaxed. It was one down and two to go. She could feel Ryan watching anxiously at her side. Deep breath. She rested the tip of her finger on the duck's dark, webbed foot and thought calm thoughts, seeing the duck, in her imagination, as a toy once more. Then, she turned the bracelet. Again she saw the flow of gold light dance between her hand and the duck, before it hugged itself around the duck's feathery body. With one last quack, the duck was back to its old, rubber self.

Just one more to go.

She reached for the puppy who stared up at her with black, saucer eyes. Then, she felt Ryan's hand on hers. 'Wait,' he said.

He picked up the puppy and cradled it against his school jumper. 'I want to keep it,' he said softly. 'Please, can I keep it?'

Chapter 5

Evie was too shocked to reply straight away.
Ryan wanted to keep the puppy? Why?
What for?

It was as though he had read her mind.
'I've always wanted a dog,' he said, the
words tumbling out fast. 'But Mum has
always said no. She says it's too much work,

57

too much responsibility. She says they need walking, but I know that. I'd look after him. Please?'

Ryan never asked for anything. He was usually so cool, so laid back. Miss Williams accused him of being half asleep most of the time. Ryan really wanted this.

But was it right?

Evie knew Ryan would take good care of the puppy, of course he would. But … she felt a familiar knot in her tummy.

'I'll call him Bob,' Ryan said with a grin. The puppy pawed Ryan's nose. 'Evie, meet Bob. Bob, meet Evie.'

'Ryan, I don't know if you should be doing this,' Evie began.

'We know what we're doing, don't we, Bob?' Ryan replied.

'He ruined the Roald Dahl,' Evie said. 'He peed on it.'

'Maybe literacy isn't his thing. I bet he's more into walks and balls and treats. Aren't you? There's a good boy.'

Evie untangled the soft toys from the wool blanket and settled them back on to cushions in the reading corner. She folded the blanket neatly and hoped Miss Williams wouldn't notice the holes. She didn't want anything to do with the damp *James and the Giant Peach*, but it was her fault, so she had to. She picked it up gingerly by the corner and dropped it into the waste paper basket.

'Hey!' Isabelle was back, waving the worksheet. 'I got Miss Williams to talk me through it so thoroughly that she ended up practically doing the whole worksheet herself. Did you two solve the animal problem?'

'Not entirely,' Evie said. 'I'd say we only managed to fix 66 per cent of the problem.'

Ryan grinned. 'Isabelle, meet Bob. Bob's coming home with me.'

When the dinner time bell went, only moments later, Evie felt relieved. Bob curled up inside Ryan's bag and the two of them disappeared out to the yard. Evie and Isabelle followed with their butty boxes.

They'd eat outdoors today – as far away
from prying eyes as possible.

They stopped by the garden planters and
the hut. It was away from the staff room
windows, so Ryan was able to let Bob
tramp through the plants. He was still only
little, so the flowers towered over him like
a jungle. He had a fantastic time trying to
catch butterflies.

'You can't keep him, you know,' Isabelle said. 'Your mum will never let you.'

'My mum doesn't have to know,' Ryan said gently. He fed Bob a triangle of ham sandwich.

'You can hardly keep him secret,' Evie said.

'Watch me.'

Bob swallowed the sandwich in three gulps.

At the end of the school day, Nana Em was waiting outside school to walk Evie and Lily home. But Evie was still thinking about Bob, who had slept the whole afternoon inside Ryan's school bag. Did that mean he

would be full of beans after his siesta and
go rampaging around Ryan's home? How on
earth would Ryan keep that a secret? And
when Ryan's mum asked where the puppy
had come from, what would he say?

Nana Em gave her a good, solid hug.
Then she said, 'What's up? You look like a
wet weekend in Blackpool.'

'Nana Em, would it be all right if I go round to Ryan's for a bit, please? Not for long. There's just something he needs a bit of help with.'

Nana Em looked thoughtful. 'I suppose it's fine. He lives on the High Street, doesn't he? Me and Lily will walk you there. It's not far back to ours, but you have to promise to be careful crossing the road.'

'I promise,' Evie said.

The High Street was clogged with cars heading out of the city, creeping forward slowly, stealing every inch of space they could manage. Buses ambled in the outside lane. A taxi beeped its horn. The shops were open and a steady stream of people wove past them, as Evie reached Ryan's. The entrance to his home was behind a dusty blue door, next to a greengrocer's. There were three buzzers and Evie pressed the one marked 'Harris'.

'Don't be long,' Nana Em said. 'It's lasagne for tea, your favourite.'

Evie nodded.

The door opened a crack. Ryan peered out, she could see one blue eye. Then the door rushed open, she was yanked inside and the door slammed behind her. 'Can't let Bob out,' Ryan said. 'The cars.'

Understandable. It was dangerous out there for a little pup who didn't know about crossing on the green man.

'How is he?' she asked.

'Brilliant!' Ryan barrelled up the stairs ahead of her and stepped into his flat. She followed, avoiding the school shoes he'd kicked off in the hall. The corridor was narrow. She wasn't sure whether to take her shoes off too. She could feel herself blushing, but Ryan came to her rescue. 'Come on through!' he called from his room.

Bob turned delighted circles when he saw Evie, and gave tiny, high-pitched yaps. His tail whipped wildly, like a propeller.

'Won't your mum hear?' Evie asked, bending down to fuss the wriggling ball of fluff. Bursts of magic popped all around Bob as he clambered to be cuddled.

'She's not home yet. It's all right, I can make this work. I've made a bed for Bob under mine. See?'

There was a little nest of towels folded under the slats of Ryan's bed. Evie could see Bob's imprint in the middle.

'And I've a water bowl. And food.'

There was an empty margarine tub full of water beside the bed, and, beside that, more ham sandwiches.

Evie sat down on the bed. The window looked out on the street below and, outside the greengrocer's, the road was as busy as ever. 'What about walks?'

'Bob will walk to school and back with me. And sleep in my bag like he did today.

He'll love running about with us all at break time too.'

Ryan's voice was so eager, so excited, that Evie couldn't say what she was really thinking: that keeping Bob a secret was a very bad idea.

Chapter 6

Evie helped Ryan as best she could. She promised to bring him an old lead of Myla's, though her spare collar would be way too big for Bob, it would be like a hula hoop around his neck. She could probably bring some of Myla's dog food too – Mum was always threatening Myla with diets.

Though Bob did seem delighted with all the sandwiches Ryan was making for him.

She tramped home, careful to cross the road safely.

Myla greeted her with huge licks all over her knees. Even Luna the cat threaded himself silkily around her ankles. Trails of happy magic hung in the air behind them. She could understand why Ryan wanted a pet. 'You two are so lovely!' she told Myla and Luna. 'I'm lucky to have you.'

'You sound better,' Mum said coming out of the dining room. 'Nana Em said you seemed peaky.'

'I'm great,' Evie said.

'Well, go and run about the garden. Tea's

in ten minutes.' Mum took Evie's school bag and dropped a kiss on to her head.

Lily was already out on the swing, kicking her legs out as far as she could. Gold light burst around the swing. 'Evie, push me! Push me!' Lily yelled.

Evie grinned. She had an even better idea. This was the perfect time to use the magic bracelet! She gripped the edge of the swing with her right hand and twisted her bracelet with her left. Straight away the swing glowed gold – and started moving of its own accord!

'Higher!' Lily yelled.

The swing pushed itself back and forth, with Lily gripping the ropes and yelling with

joy. Gold light streamed from them both like a tail. Sometimes it was really nice to be an older sister – sometimes.

'Higher!' Lily called.

'That's as high as it goes unless you want to land up in space,' Evie cried with a laugh.

'As high as the sky!' Lily insisted.

'Woo-hoo!' Evie cried.

'Evie.' Mum's voice from inside the house was stern. Angry.

Evie caught the swing. She twisted her bracelet quickly. All traces of gold light vanished. Lily dragged her feet on the ground, stopping the swing.

'Evie Hall, come here, please.'

Uh-oh. It was never good when Mum

73

used her full name. Had she pushed Lily too high? Or maybe Mum had found out about Bob? Or worse, about the bracelet?

Evie hung her head as she crept towards the back door.

Mum was just inside, holding Evie's school bag in one hand and a white slip of paper in the other.

The letter from Miss Williams.

Evie had forgotten all about it, what with Bob and everything. She'd just shoved it into her book bag alongside her butty box. Which Mum had been looking for when she found the letter.

'A detention? How did that happen?' Mum asked.

Evie stared at her feet. Her school shoes were shined, her socks still pulled up to her knees. She looked neat and tidy and well-behaved. But it was just a show. She knew she'd let Mum and Dad down.

'I'm sorry. I scribbled on my desk.'

'Oh, Evie. Why?'

Evie shrugged. She had no answer that
Mum was going to believe.

'Well, I'm going to talk to Dad about this
as soon as he's home from work and we'll
decide a punishment together. I'm very
disappointed in you.'

Tea, after that, was a very gloomy one.
Lily wittered on about her day and all
the scrapes she'd got into. Some were real
scrapes and she had the scabs on her knees
to prove it. Others were just disagreements
with her classmates.

But Evie hardly spoke. She pushed her
pasta around with her fork. Mum and Dad
always wanted them to clean their plates,
but she just wasn't hungry. She forced

down a few mouthfuls before asking to be excused.

'Fine,' Mum agreed, 'but your dad and I will be up to talk to you as soon as we've decided. OK?'

Evie nodded glumly.

She threw herself on her bed and kicked off her shoes. Today had started so well, with a new bracelet from Grandma Iris and the promise of magic, but now it was all horrible.

And magic was to blame. Magic made the pencil dance and the toy animals become real ones and it was magic's fault that she'd had to bring the letter home.

Maybe she should take her bracelet off

and never do magic again?

She pulled up her sleeve and looked at the band of shells.

But it was a gift from Grandma.

She had no idea what to do for the best.

'I thought she was settling in so well.'

Evie sat up. She could hear Dad speaking downstairs, in the hallway. His voice was so gravelly, the sound of it carried all the way up the stairs to her room. Mum was harder to hear, but she must be telling Dad about the letter.

'Why did she do that?' Dad asked.

Mum said something back.

'Is she unhappy do you think? Or maybe it's her new friends. Isabelle and Ryan, is it?

Maybe they're a bad influence?'

Evie moved over to the door. She could just make out Mum's words now.

'... don't think she's unhappy. She hasn't said so. Maybe it is her friends. Maybe we have to do something about them?'

No! Evie felt her heart thump in her chest. Mum couldn't stop her seeing Isabelle and Ryan. They were her best friends! What would she do without them?

She heard Dad's footsteps on the stairs, heading up to her attic room. She sat neatly on the bed, head up, hands in her lap. Dad could be strict, but he was fair. He wouldn't stop her seeing her friends, she was sure.

The door opened.

Dad was still in his work boiler suit, wood dust settled in the creases of the fabric. He looked stern. 'Evie, I've seen your letter home. I don't want anything like this to happen again, is that clear?'

Evie nodded.

'There will be no screens for a week. No TV, no computer, no tablet. Understood?'

Evie nodded again.

He was waiting. Was he going to say anything about Isabelle and Ryan?

The silence continued.

Then she realised what he was waiting for. 'I'm sorry,' she said quickly.

'Good. Mum will be in soon to tuck you in. Sleep tight.' He stamped a quick kiss on her forehead.

The door closed.

Evie had a feeling she hadn't heard the last of it.

Chapter 7

Evie dropped the signed letter silently on to
Miss Williams' desk. No screens for a week
was a long punishment for something that
hadn't even been her fault. Still, at least Dad
hadn't said anything else about Isabelle and
Ryan being a bad influence.

As she walked past Ryan's desk, Evie

couldn't help but notice his smile. It was highly, suspiciously angelic. He sat patiently, waiting for Miss Williams to begin lessons, his uniform was neat, and his hair was brushed flat instead of spiked up with gel, like usual. Ryan Harris was not himself.

What was going on?

'Are you all right?' she whispered.

He nodded, eagerly. Too eagerly.

Isabelle leaned across her desk and said, 'He's got Bob in his bag. He's going for Perfect Schoolboy of the Year, so that Miss Williams won't notice the extra pupil in the classroom.'

Ryan gave her a quick wink.

Ha!

She flicked a glance down to his bag. The zip was open a tiny bit and a little black, shiny nose snuffled up. She heard an excited yip, as Bob recognised her scent.

'Hush,' Ryan whispered. 'Remember you're a secret!'

Bob must have listened, because his nose disappeared into the bag and he was perfectly silent for the first session of the day.

When they were allowed to barrel out into the yard at break, Ryan was right in front, with Bob still nestled in his bag. Evie hurried after him.

'Are you going to let the dog out of the bag?' Evie asked with a grin.

85

Ryan glanced at the staff room window. There was no one there watching.

Evie could tell he was tempted, and it wasn't good for Bob to stay inside the stuffy bag all day. 'We could take him to the shed, to run around there. That's out of the way,' she suggested.

Ryan headed to the vegetable planters, cradling his bag carefully. As soon as he put it on the ground and unzipped it, Bob leapt out. He raced around the shed delightedly, woofing and yipping at every single exciting thing. Ryan was right on his tail. 'Good boy! Who's a good boy?' Ryan said.

Evie joined in the chase. Soon, all three of them tore around, getting out of breath and filled with laughter. Bob panted happily as he crashed into ankles and bounded over feet. Joyous magic swirled around them all, Evie trailed her hands through it. It felt light as air, but soft and warm too.

Where was Isabelle? Why was she missing out on the fun?

Evie stopped cantering and looked for her friend.

Isabelle strolled out of the school building towards them. She was carrying something small and fluffy. When she got close, Evie saw that she carried the toy kitten from reading corner.

'Evie,' Isabelle said, 'I was wondering if you could give me a pet too? I was thinking this kitten.' She held up the toy expectantly.

Evie frowned. 'I don't know. What would you say to your mum and dad?'

'You're worrying about nothing. They won't mind. They give me anything I ask for. As long as I ask for it often enough.'

'Then why don't you ask them for a real kitten?' Evie clasped her hands together tightly. She hated saying no to Isabelle.

'Because I want a magic kitten. You gave Ryan a magic puppy.' Isabelle folded her arms and looked cross.

'To be fair, I didn't give a magic puppy to Ryan, he just wouldn't let me change it back. That's not the same thing. And now he's running around with Bob at school and

it's only a matter of time before someone
notices and then he'll have to say where Bob
came from and then everyone will find out
about the magic, and then they'll take the
bracelets away and we'll never get to use
magic ever, ever, ever again.' Evie's words
rushed out in a flood. She hadn't meant to
tell Isabelle all her worries, but they all just
bubbled up out of her.

Isabelle held the kitten up and waggled
its front paws at Evie. 'Don't worry, Evie,'
Isabelle said in a kitteny kind of voice, 'it's
all going to be OK.'

Just then, they heard a yip and a howl.
Bob had got himself tangled up in a stray
skipping rope and had tumbled head-over-

heels. Ryan scooped him up. 'Careful!'

Isabelle lowered the toy kitten. 'Oops.
Maybe it won't be fine,' she said. 'You're
right. Ryan is asking for trouble.' She
marched over to Ryan and stood with the
kitten shoved under her arm. 'Ryan. Evie
thinks you should come clean about Bob. So
do I. You should tell your mum.'

'No way!' Ryan cradled Bob to his chest.
'My mum would never let him stay. He's not
doing any harm. You're just jealous, because
I've got something I've always wanted and
you haven't.'

Evie gasped. That was a horrible thing for
Ryan to say.

Isabelle didn't even reply. She turned on
her heel and stalked back into the school
building.

'Isabelle!' Evie called, but Isabelle didn't
look back.

Ryan blushed, but said nothing. He
cuddled Bob and walked away from Evie.

Evie didn't know what to do.

Isabelle and Ryan didn't speak to each other all of the rest of the afternoon. It was as if a frozen wall had been built between them. Evie, whose desk was near the window, watched them anxiously, but there was no sign of a thaw.

When the bell rang at the end of the school day, they both stomped out, without saying goodbye to each other.

Was there anything she could do to help? She tried to think of magic she might perform – would it make it better if Isabelle did get a kitten? Or the clothes she'd asked for from her sister's wardrobe?

'Come on, slowcoach,' Nana Em said as they walked home, 'you'll get left behind.'

Evie hardly noticed the people in the High Street as they hurried home. All she could think about was the frost between Ryan and Isabelle.

She was the same at home. Even playing with Lily and Myla couldn't take her mind off it completely. Myla made her laugh when she put her paws up on the swing, as though she wanted a turn. And Luna the cat was funny, curling into a flower pot in the warm sun. But, when she wasn't laughing, the memory of the freeze between her friends rushed back, like an ice cube slipped down her back.

Then, before Mum and Dad got home, the phone rang. Lily rushed to answer it, but it was for Evie.

'Hello?' Evie said into the receiver.

'Evie? It's Ryan.' He sounded odd. Frightened.

'What's wrong?'

'It's Bob. I left him in the flat by himself

while I had to go and meet my dad for tea. I've just got back now. My bedroom is a chewed up mess, and I can't find Bob anywhere. He's gone!'

'Oh, no, Ryan. I'm sorry.'

'Can you help? I don't know who else to ask. Can you help me look for him?'

'Of course I can. I'll be there right away.'

Chapter 8

'You can go to Ryan's until tea time,' Nana
Em said. 'But your mum and dad aren't best
pleased with you right now, so don't be late!'

'I won't. Thank you!' Evie gave Nana Em
a quick hug, and then raced out of the front
door. Where had Bob got to? Was he safe?
Had Ryan's mum come home to find the

mess Bob had made?

She was out of breath from running by the time she pressed the buzzer, but she'd got there in record time.

Ryan looked pale and grey when he opened the door.

'Any sign?' Evie asked.

He shook his head.

She followed him upstairs and through to his room. He hadn't been exaggerating. It looked as though a tiny whirlwind had battered his bedroom – socks were mangled, his bedclothes had been pulled on to the floor, books and magazines were missing whole chunks. And there was a little yellow puddle on the old grate.

'Oh dear,' Evie said.

'What's worse is he's not here,' Ryan
replied.

'I'll tidy this up before your mum gets
home. You look for him in every corner of
the flat. OK?'

'I have looked for him. We need to widen

the search, we need to head outside.'

'But this needs to be fixed.' She waved at the room. There was only one thing to do. 'You have to phone Isabelle to come and help too,' she said.

Ryan pressed his lips tighter and shook his head.

'You have to. We need all the help we can get.' Evie stood in the middle of the floor, her feet set wide apart. This was important. He had to listen to her. 'Ryan, you need to phone Isabelle right now, and tell her you're sorry for what you said. You have to do it because Bob needs you to. Three of us stand a better chance of finding him than just two. So go and pick up the phone.'

Ryan threw his hand up. 'Fine. Fine. I'll do it.' He turned to leave the room, but paused before he was out. 'And, Evie,' he said softly, 'thanks.'

She busied herself with the mess while Ryan was on the phone in the hallway. The duvet went back on the bed and the books were tidied into a pile – there was nothing she could do about the nibbled corners. She found some newspapers in the kitchen recycling to mop up the yellow puddle.

Ryan didn't say anything when he got back. Was Isabelle coming to help? What had she said? Had Ryan apologised?

Ryan pulled out Bob's bed from under his own. 'Bob? Bob, where are you?' he said.

Questions would have to wait. They had a puppy to find.

Where would she go if she were an inquisitive puppy exploring his new home? Well, she knew where Myla would go – the kitchen! There were crisps and crackers, biscuits and bananas, and where there was food, there was Myla!

Evie rushed straight to the kitchen. Was Bob busy munching his way through the cupboards?

She opened every door, but there was no sign of the little pup.

She moved on to the bathroom, which was damp with wet towels hanging over the bath. No dog. Ryan's mum's room was cold, but smelled of her perfume. No dog. The living room was cosy, with blankets and rugs, thrown higgledy-piggledy over the backs of the two sofas. But there was no sign of Bob.

The buzzer rang.

Isabelle!

Evie dashed downstairs.

Isabelle looked a bit sulky, standing in the doorway, but at least she was there.

Ryan's footsteps were heavy on the stairs behind her. 'Good, the reinforcements are here. We need to extend the parameters of our search area, and reconnoitre the external perimeters.'

'I've no idea *what* you're on about,'

Isabelle said. 'What's the magic word?'

'Sorry? No, is it please? No, it's sorry,' Ryan stumbled.

'Both will do just fine,' Isabelle said. 'What do you need me to do?'

'Search the street,' Ryan replied.

'Roger that,' Isabelle said, clicking her heels together. They were friends again! Evie felt a little fizz of pleasure. Bob was still missing, but at least Ryan and Isabelle had made up after their fight.

Ryan suddenly looked upset. 'I thought I shut the door behind me, but maybe I didn't. I was excited about seeing Dad. He drove all the way to the city to see me today. Maybe Bob followed me out. He's so little, I might not have noticed.'

They all looked out at the road.

Even after six o'clock it was still busy.
Cars and taxis, buses and bicycles crawled
past. The air shimmered with the fumes
from their exhausts. Horns blared when
two passed too close together. It was no
place for a puppy.

'Bob!' Ryan called.

They all joined in, circling around the
flat's entrance, calling Bob's name.

'Do you think something happened
to him?' Isabelle whispered to Evie. She
pointed at the road.

'No!' Evie said quickly. 'No! That would
be awful. We have to find him.'

The greengrocer below Ryan's flat was closing for the evening. He was carrying big tubs of apples and peaches from the table outside back into the cool dark of the shop. Ryan checked as many tubs as he could – but Bob wasn't nestled in with the nectarines.

'Bob! Bob!' Evie called. She checked behind lamp-posts and behind the postbox, but there was no sign.

Isabelle ducked to see under the parked cars along the edge of the street, calling as she went.

But there was no answering yap, or scurry of tiny claws along the pavement. No wagging tail or panting tongue. It was as though Bob had disappeared.

'Can you use magic to help?' Isabelle asked, wiping dust off her knees.

'I don't know. How?' Evie asked. She'd do anything she could to help find Bob.

But Isabelle had no suggestion to make.

It was getting late, nearly tea time. If they

didn't find Bob soon then Evie would have to leave to get home. She really, really didn't want to do that.

But it looked as though she was going to have to. Bob wasn't in the street outside the flat.

Where could he have got to?

And then she heard a tiny, frightened bark.

'Listen!' Isabelle said. They all stood stock still. And the sound came again. *Yip! Yip!*

'Bob!' Ryan beamed.

'But where?' Isabelle asked.

Yip! Yip!

The sound was coming from above their heads. Evie looked up. She was looking at the underside of a stripy awning. It stretched out above the greengrocer's, sheltering the fruit and veg from the sun. And she could see, in the middle of the awning, the imprint of a tiny little body. The shape moved, and she could see that its tail was wagging.

They'd found Bob! He was on top of the awning. How on earth had he got there?

More importantly, how on earth were they going to get him down?

Chapter 9

Evie looked up at Bob's little body, cradled by the awning. How was he going to get down?

She stepped back and tried to see Bob, but the road meant she couldn't step out far enough to get a good view.

The yip sound turned to frightened whimpers.

'I know what's above the awning!'
Ryan said excitedly. 'It's Mum's bedroom
window.'

They raced back up to the flat, and into
Ryan's mum's room. There was a bed, and a
wardrobe, and below the window, a dressing
table and stool. Bob must have scrambled
up the stool, on to the table and towards the
window – which was open just a fraction, to
let in fresh air.

All three shot across to the window.

'Help me move the dressing table, we need
to reach out to get him,' Ryan said.

They hoisted the dressing table out of the
way. Bottles and jars clinked and swayed,
but nothing fell. Ryan pulled the window

open wide and they all looked out. It was a crush, but they each wanted to see how Bob was doing.

The little puppy was shivering. His ears were down and his tiny tail was tucked between his legs. He tried to scamper towards them, but the awning was slippery and he slid right back to where he'd started.

'Can we reach him?' Isabelle stretched out as far as she could, her fingers splayed wide.

'Careful!' Ryan gripped the back of her jumper. 'Don't lean too far, that awning isn't strong enough to hold you.'

It was true, the awning was just thin plastic. It wasn't meant for walking on – not even by puppies.

'We can't go out there,' Evie said.

'We have to save him!' Ryan said fiercely.

'Of course, but how?' Evie asked.

They all looked around the room, their eyes darting from the woven floor rug, to the books on the bedside table, to the dressing gown on the back of the door.

'I've got it!' Isabelle said. 'Evie makes the

rug come alive – like a flying carpet! And we
fly out and rescue Bob.'

Evie shook her head quickly. 'I've been
doing little bits of magic, but I don't know
if I could control a flying carpet this high
above the ground. What if the carpet sends
us soaring, or just drops us in the path of
a bus?'

Isabelle nodded thoughtfully. 'Well, when
you put it like that, you've got a point.'

'We need a fishing net, or a giant scoop,
or something like that,' Evie said, looking
at Ryan.

He shrugged hopelessly. 'There isn't
anything like that here. I've got a fishing net,
but it's at my dad's house. That's near a river.'

'The dressing gown!' Evie said. 'It's got a hood. We can lower it out, with a ham sandwich in the hood as bait. Bob will climb in, I'm sure, and then we can haul him back to safety.'

'Brilliant!' Ryan said. 'I'll go and make a sandwich. You tell Bob we're coming for him.'

Ryan headed to the kitchen, while Evie and Isabelle tried to soothe Bob. 'You'll be back with us in two shakes of a pup's tail,' Isabelle told him.

When he came back, Ryan was holding the most speedily made sandwich ever – it was just a piece of ham and a slice of bread rolled together. He lifted his mum's

116

dressing gown from its hook on the back of the door. The gown was made of shiny, slidey fabric. Evie wondered, for a short second, whether it was a good idea to put a ham sandwich in something so pretty. But then she thought, it was for Bob. They had no choice.

Ryan popped the bait in place, and lowered the gown gently from the window, keeping a tight grip on the bottom hem. It slithered towards Bob. He sniffed the air and licked his lips. His nose twitched, his ears pricked up. His tail started wagging.

'Get the sandwich, there's a good boy!' Ryan said.

Bob took a few tentative steps towards

the hood. He sniffed. His front paws
stepped inside.

'Go on, Bob, you can do it,' Isabelle
urged him.

Bob licked the sandwich.

'One more step,' Evie said. 'Please, Bob,
go on.'

Bob lunged forwards, into the hood. He
bit down on the sandwich in delight. Ryan
tugged at the fabric in his hands. Bob jerked
at the sudden movement, but he was so
interested in the meal that he didn't step out
of the hood. Ryan dragged the gown gently,
back towards the window. Bob came along
with it.

When he was within reach, Isabelle leaned

out and scooped Bob into her hands.

'Hurray!' Evie said.

'Ryan!' the voice came from the doorway. There was a woman standing there. She had the same blue eyes as Ryan and her blonde hair was pulled back off her face. She had to be Ryan's mum.

'Ryan,' his mum said, 'why is there a sandwich in my dressing gown? And why is there a puppy in my bedroom?'

Chapter 10

Ryan coughed. He looked down at the ground. Then up at the ceiling. He was trying not to look at his mum.

'Ryan?' she asked, very firmly indeed.

'Maybe we should go, Ms Harris,' Isabelle said brightly. 'It's getting on.'

'No, Isabelle, I think you should probably

stay right there. And Ryan should start talking,' Ms Harris replied.

Evie wondered how on earth Ryan would get out of this.

He let out a deep sigh. 'Mum, this is Bob.' He laid the gown carefully on the dresser and took Bob from Isabelle's cupped hands.

Bob wriggled in delight at being safely reunited with Ryan. Evie saw wisps of magic light float up from his wagging tail.

Ryan held Bob out to his mum.

'Whose dog is Bob?' Ms Harris asked.

'He's my dog,' Ryan said sheepishly. 'He's been living here since yesterday, but he climbed out of the window. We rescued him with your dressing gown. Sorry. There's crumbs on it now.'

'Oh dear.' Ms Harris sat down heavily on her bed. She eyed Bob warily. Then she reached out a fingertip and Bob licked it. She gave Bob a tiny smile. 'Ryan, he's lovely, but he can't stay here.'

'But, Mum—'

'But, nothing. This is no place for a dog. The road is too busy, there's no garden to play in – it isn't fair on Bob.'

Evie felt tears sting her eyes. She knew, deep down, that Ms Harris was right, but that didn't stop her hurting for Ryan. He loved Bob, just like she loved Myla and Luna. Having to say goodbye to him was horrible.

Ryan held Bob close to his chest and leaned his face against the little dog's fur.

'There's no room here,' Ms Harris continued, 'but there might be room at your dad's. He lives in the countryside.'

What?

Evie felt a prickle of hope. Was she hearing right?

Ms Harris took out her phone. 'Wait here. I'm going to make a call.' She left the room, already tapping her screen.

They could only hear muffled words from the kitchen. Isabelle stood close to Ryan with her fingers crossed tightly and her eyes screwed shut. Evie rested her hand on his shoulder, to let him know she was there.

Bob had curled up against Ryan's chest and was fast asleep after his adventure on the awning.

Moments later, Ms Harris was back – and she was smiling properly now! 'Your dad says yes! Bob can go and live at his house. Dad's still in the city. He'll pick Bob up before he heads home. You'll be able to see

Bob every weekend. How does that sound?'

Ryan was so pleased he couldn't speak.
Tears glistened in his eyes. 'Thank you,' he
finally managed to whisper.

'It's all right,' Isabelle said cheerfully.
'What are friends for?'

Evie wasn't entirely sure that Ryan had
been thanking them, but she had been happy
to help.

Oh!

Except she was supposed to be back
before tea time! Was she late? She checked
her watch.

'Oh no,' she said. 'I'm supposed to be
home!'

She was already being punished for

the detention. If she was late home too,
then Mum and Dad would really think
Isabelle and Ryan were a bad influence.
She remembered what Dad had said, that
he and Mum would have to do something
about her friends.

'Evie, is it?' Ms Harris asked kindly. 'How
about I ring your mum right now and tell
her that you've been busy rescuing our dog?
Do you think that would help?'

Evie nodded frantically. That would
definitely help.

She told Ms Harris the number.

She kept her fingers crossed that it would
be enough. She really couldn't bear for Mum
and Dad to be cross again.

Evie could hear Mum's voice, saying 'yes' and 'mm-hm' while Ms Harris explained where she was. There was a long pause, while Ms Harris listened, a serious look on her face. Then, she disconnected.

'That was interesting,' Ms Harris said.

'"Interesting" doesn't mean good,' Isabelle said. 'Miss Williams says my homework is interesting before giving me a D.'

Ms Harris laughed. 'No. It really was interesting. Don't worry, Evie, your mum understands that you had to help rescue Bob. But she also said that she's been meaning to do something about your friends.'

Oh no.

'She thinks that it's high time she got to

128

know them a bit better. So, we're all invited
for tea at your house tomorrow. What do
you think of that?'

Evie could have clapped she was so happy.
Isabelle did clap. Bursts of magic showered
from her hands, gold glitter that only they
could see.

Bob wriggled in Ryan's arms, woken by the noise.

He'd have a good home at Ryan's dad's. And Ryan would see him all the time when he went to visit. And Mum wasn't worried about her friends being a bad influence, she just wanted to get to know them better.

Evie smiled. Perhaps the magic had gone just right, after all.

Evie and friends

Evie

Full name: Evie Hall

Lives in: Sheffield

Family: Mum, Dad, younger sister Lily

Pets: Chocolate Labrador Myla and cat Luna

Favourite foods: rice, peas and chicken – lasagna – and chocolate bourbon biscuits!

Best thing about Evie: friendly and determined!

Isabelle

Full name: Isabelle Carter

Lives in: Sheffield

Family: Mum, Dad, older sister Lizzie

Favourite foods: sweet treats – and anything spicy!

Best thing about Isabelle: she's the life and soul of the party!

Ryan

Full name: Ryan Harris

Lives in: Sheffield

Family: lives with his mum, visits his dad

Pets: would love a dog …

Favourite foods: Marmite, chocolate – and anything with pasta!

Best thing about Ryan: easy-going, and fun to be with!

Who's your Magic Bracelet perfect pet?

Take this quiz to find out
which pet is perfect for you!

What's your favourite way to spend a day?

A. ❑ Walking in the hills.

B. ■ Curled up in the sun with a good
adventure story.

C. ❑ A swim in the river – I'm a real water
baby!

What's your favourite food?

A. ❑ Roast beef with all the trimmings!

B. ❑ Fish finger sandwich for me.

C. ■ Anything – I'm a bit of an omnivore!

What kind of friend are you?

A. ☐ I'm loyal and devoted!
B. ☐ I like to take my time before I'm sure who my friends are.
C. ■ Hanging out with friends and family in a big group is the best!

And where do you live?

A. ■ Right next to a big park.
B. ☐ A snug and cosy flat, with plenty of bean bags and pillows.
C. ☐ On a farm!

Mostly A
Your perfect pet is: *a dog!*

Mostly B
Your perfect pet is: *a kitten!*

Mostly C
Your perfect pet is: *a duck!*

Can you find all the words?

BRACELET ISABELLE
FRIENDS MAGIC
LILY EVIE
RYAN KITTEN
ENCHANTED PUPPY

Jessica Ennis-Hill grew up in Sheffield with her parents and younger sister. She has been World and European heptathlon champion and won gold at the London 2012 Olympics and silver at Rio 2016. She still lives in Sheffield and enjoys reading stories to her son every night.

You can find Jessica on Twitter **@J_Ennis**, on Facebook, and on Instagram **@jessicaennishill**

Jessica says: *'I have so many great memories of being a kid. My friends and I spent lots of time exploring and having adventures where my imagination used to run riot! It has been so much fun working with Elen Caldecott to go back to that world of stories and imagination. I hope you'll enjoy them too!'*

Elen Caldecott co-wrote the Evie's Magic Bracelet stories with Jessica. Elen lives in Totterdown, in Bristol – chosen mainly because of the cute name. She has written several warm, funny books about ordinary children doing extraordinary things.

You can find out more at
www.elencaldecott.com